DIRTY
GERT

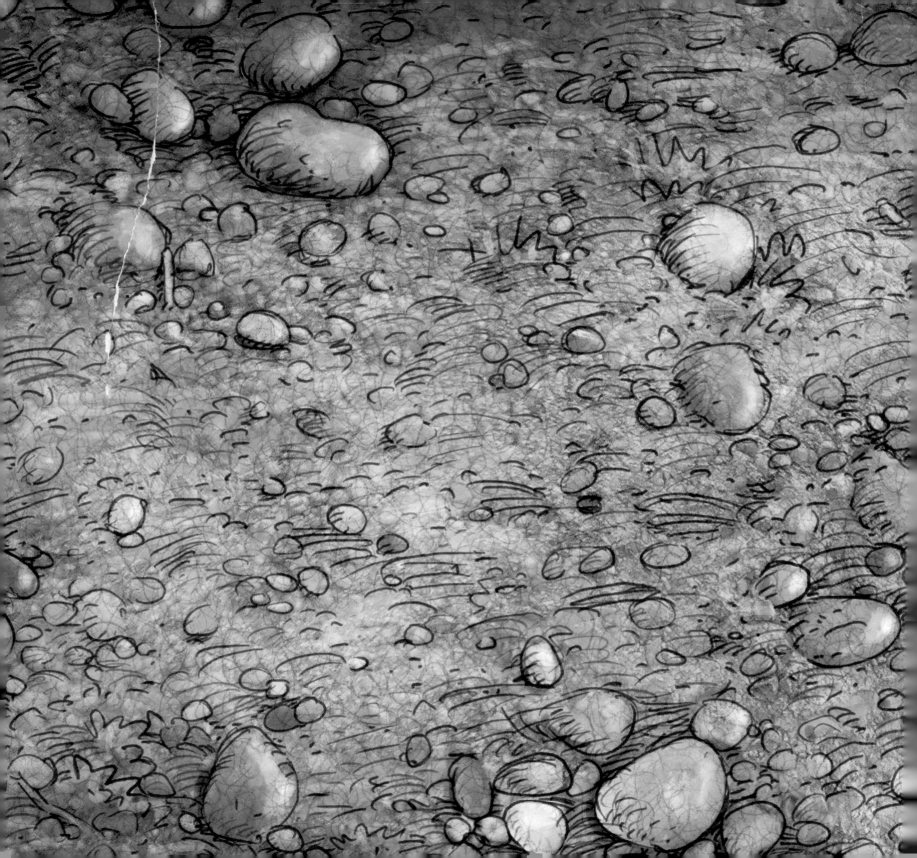

DIRTY GERT

Tedd Arnold

Holiday House / New York

For "Dirty Diane"—
She lives on it. She plays with it.
She plants it. She paints with it!
In Diane's hands, it's exquisite!

Library of Congress Cataloging-in-Publication Data
Arnold, Tedd.
Dirty Gert / by Tedd Arnold. — 1st ed.
p. cm.
Summary: Little Gert loves to play in the dirt so much that she turns into a tree.
ISBN 978-0-8234-2404-7 (hardcover)
[1. Stories in rhyme. 2. Trees—Fiction. 3. Humorous stories.] I. Title.
PZ8.3.A647Di 2013
[E]—dc23
2012006578

ISBN 978-0-8234-3054-3 (paperback)

Little Gert loved eating dirt.
The worms all idolized her.

But how did she first get to be
A soil internalizer?

She rolled in it.
She dug in it.

Look at her go!

She tasted it.
Didn't even spit!
It seemed to energize her.

Mom and Dad did not get mad.
They simply supervised her.

As years went by, they'd try and try,
But could not civilize her.

Hold up your pinkie like this.

And then one day she went to play
When no one was the wiser.

A rainstorm hit, and quickly it
Completely moisturized her.

She sprouted and

She shouted and
Her food reorganized her!

WHOA!

Quite soon she found herself root-bound.
It happily surprised her.

Ruby May came out to play
But didn't recognize her.

The neighbors thought that someone ought
To scrub and sanitize her.

Her brother, Matt, decided that
He needed to disguise her.

Her best friend, Dwight, thought that he might
At least deodorize her.

The local news sent camera crews.
They filmed and televised her.

The lawyers called. They were appalled!
No one had legalized her.

Zoologists and botanists
And doctors analyzed her.

Soon all the ruckus,
All the fuss,
Began to traumatize her.

First came her wilt
And then her tilt!
Her fame had jeopardized her!

But Mom and Dad,
They're smart and true.
They always knew
Just what to do.

They trimmed and fertilized her!